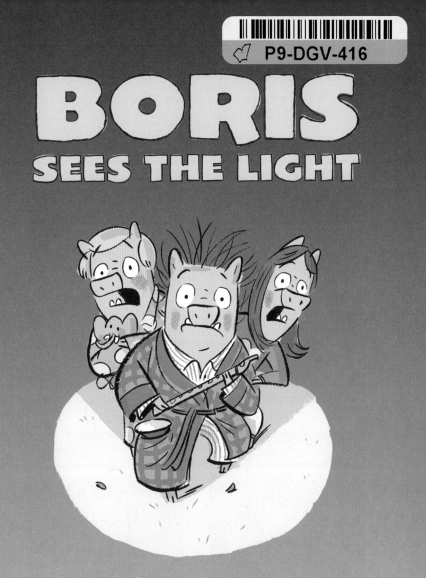

BORIS
SEES THE LIGHT

by Andrew Joyner

BRANCHES

SCHOLASTIC INC.

ADVENTURES ARE ALWAYS JUST AROUND THE CORNER WITH BORIS!

Table of Contents

Introduction.................................... 1

Chapter One................................. 9

Chapter Two 19

Chapter Three................................31

Chapter Four 39

Chapter Five 47

Chapter Six 52

Chapter Seven................................61

How to Make a Shadow Portrait.....69

No part of this publication may be reproduced, stored in a retrieval system, or transmitted in any form or by any means, electronic, mechanical, photocopying, recording, or otherwise, without written permission of the publisher. For information regarding permission, write to Puffin Books, a division of Penguin Group (Australia), 250 Camberwell Road, Camberwell, Victoria 3124, Australia.

Library of Congress Cataloging-in-Publication Data

Joyner, Andrew.
Boris sees the light / Andrew Joyner.
p. cm.
Originally published: Camberwell, Victoria, Australia : Puffin, 2011.
Summary: Boris and his friends Frederick and Alice are camping in the backyard, but it is very dark—except for a mysterious light moving through the bushes.
ISBN 978-0-545-48453-4 — ISBN 978-0-545-48454-1 1.
Warthog—Juvenile fiction. 2. Camping—Juvenile fiction. 3.
Sleepovers—Juvenile fiction. 4. Friendship—Juvenile fiction. [1.
Warthog—Fiction. 2. Camping—Fiction. 3. Sleepovers—Fiction. 4.
Friendship—Fiction.] I. Title.
PZ7.J8573Bou 2013
823.92—dc23
2013003045
ISBN 978-0-545-48453-4 (hardcover) / ISBN 978-0-545-48454-1 (paperback)

12 11 10 9 8 7 6 5 4 3 2   13 14 15 16 17 18/0

Printed in China   38
First Scholastic printing, October 2013

Meet Boris.
He's a lot like you.

favorite robe

favorite toothbrush

favorite book
(this week)

favorite flashlight

favorite sleeping bag

favorite pajamas

He lives in an old bus.

This is Mom.

This is Dad.

He takes care of his pets.

Boris likes his friends to come over.

This is Alice.

This is Frederick.

And he likes to dream.

Boris dreams of big skies.

He dreams of big rides.

And big songs.

But mostly he dreams
about big adventures!

You'll never be bored when Boris is around!
So hitch a ride for his next adventure.
He could take you anywhere ...
across a desert,
onto a spaceship, or maybe
just around the corner.

CHAPTER ONE

Boris was putting up his tent.

Alice and Frederick
were sleeping over.

They were going to camp
in Boris's backyard.

Boris put Alice and Frederick
to work. And soon everything
was ready.

Dad helped them light a campfire.

Mom helped them forage for food.

And then it was time to eat.

The toasted marshmallows were a big hit. Especially with Boris's sheep, Frank.

CHAPTER TWO

After dinner they sang songs.

Frederick played his recorder.

As the sun set they started an epic game of hide-and-seek.

And then
it was bedtime.

It was a close contest. But Alice won.

Boris and his friends had lots of fun
in the tent.

Or we could
do something else.

Boris thought for a minute. And
then he had a great idea.

How about a story?

He knew just the one to tell.

CHAPTER THREE

Frederick yawned.

Frederick often yawned
when he felt nervous.

The moon shone through the trees,
making strange shadows on the
wall of the tent.

The tent door flapped and
cracked in the night wind.

And then Boris was all alone.

He waited for Alice to come back.
It felt like a long time.

That's when he heard it.

CHAPTER FOUR

He couldn't see them anywhere.

They must be inside.

As Boris walked toward the bus
he saw a light moving around
near the fence.

Then something grabbed his leg.

It was Alice. She was hiding in the
bushes with Frederick.

What's that light?

Or the single, glowing eye of a giant zombie monster.

We can't stay here all night.

I'm going to see what it is.

Alice and Frederick weren't sure that was a good idea. But they couldn't let Boris go out there alone.

CHAPTER FIVE

The light was moving everywhere.

It shone up and then down.
It shone left and then right.

The wind shook the trees.
It blew through the recorder.

The light stopped.

49

And then it started to move again.

Straight toward Boris and
Frederick and Alice.

CHAPTER SIX

The light spoke.

It was Mr. Blume,
Boris's neighbor.

I thought I heard something.

55

Mr. Blume gave them each
a turn with the helmet.

He told them about some
of his caving adventures.

And then it was time
to say good night.

Nice to see you, Boris. Delighted to meet you, Frederick and Alice.

CHAPTER SEVEN

Boris and Frederick and Alice
walked back to the tent.

The night was still dark.

The wind was still blowing.

And the shadows were still spooky.

Frederick shivered.

It's getting cold out here.

We could find
a warmer spot.

THE END

HOW TO MAKE A
SHADOW
PORTRAIT
BY BORIS

THINGS YOU NEED:

1. A friend or family member to model for your portrait. I'm using Alice!

2. A chair

3. A lamp

4. A large piece of paper

5. Masking tape

6. A pencil

7. Scissors

8. A thick black marker or paint

Now turn the page... 69

STEP 1: Place your chair in front of a wall. Ask your model to sit sideways in the chair.

STEP 2: Tape your piece of paper to the wall, behind your model.

STEP 3: Get an adult to help you with this next step. Shine the lamp onto your model so it makes a clear shadow of their profile in the paper. You might need to move the lamp around to get the shadow you want.

STEP 4: Ask your model to sit *VERY STILL.* Carefully trace around their shadow in pencil. This will give you an outline of their head and shoulders on your piece of paper.

Now turn the page...

STEP 5: Take down your paper and cut around the pencil outline with your scissors.

STEP 6: Color in your cutout with a black marker or paint.

NOW YOU'VE MADE A SHADOW PORTRAIT!

Another word for a shadow portrait is SILHOUETTE.

YOU'LL NEVER BE BORED WHEN BORIS IS AROUND! LOOK FOR HIS OTHER EXCITING ADVENTURES!

He lives with his mom and dad in a van that once traveled all over the world. But now it never leaves the yard. If only it could take him on an adventure . . . to the jungles of the Amazon or on a wild African safari.

Then one morning, Boris feels a jolt. Could it be? Is the van really moving? Is Boris on the adventure of his dreams at last?

Boris loves pets! He already has lots of them. All he's missing is his favorite animal, a Komodo dragon—the biggest lizard in the world!

When Boris pretends that he's getting one, everyone in his class wants to see it. Uh-oh! Boris needs to come up with a plan . . . fast. Luckily, he's got his friends by his side and a trick up his sleeve!